BEAUTY
and the
BEAST

AN INTERACTIVE FAIRY TALE ADVENTURE

by Matt Doeden

illustrated by
Sabrina Miramon

CAPSTONE PRESS
a capstone imprint

You Choose Books are published by Capstone Press,
1710 Roe Crest Drive, North Mankato, Minnesota 56003
www.mycapstone.com

Library of Congress Cataloging-in-Publication Data
Names: Doeden, Matt, author. | Miramon, Sabrina, illustrator. Title: Beauty and
the beast : an interactive fairy tale adventure / by Matt Doeden; illustrated by
Sabrina Miramon. Description: North Mankato, Minnesota : You Choose Books, an
imprint of Capstone Press, [2018] | Series: You choose books. Fractured fairy tales |
Summary: A choose-your-own-adventure in which the reader can proceed as a
knight facing a female beast, explore the future with an android prince, or chase
superstardom in a modern version of the classic fairy tale. Includes a history of Beauty
and the Beast. Identifiers: LCCN 2018018478 (print) | LCCN 2018024423 (ebook)
| ISBN 9781543530117 (eBook PDF) | ISBN 9781543530070 (hardcover) | ISBN
9781543530094 (pbk.) Subjects: LCSH: Plot-your-own stories. | CYAC: Fairy
tales. | Knights and knighthood—Fiction. | Monsters—Fiction. | Princes—Fiction.
| Robots—Fiction. | Singers—Fiction. | Plot-your-own stories. Classification: LCC
PZ8.D6663 (ebook) | LCC PZ8.D6663 Be 2018 (print) | DDC [Fic]—dc23 LC
record available at https://lccn.loc.gov/2018018478

Editorial Credits
Michelle Hasselius, editor; Heidi Thompson, designer; Jo Miller, media researcher;
Tori Abraham, production specialist

Image Credits
Shutterstock: solarbird, background

Printed in Canada.
PA020

TABLE OF
CONTENTS

ABOUT YOUR ADVENTURE

YOU are about to enter a tale of fantasy, fear, love, and friendship. It's the classic tale of *Beauty and the Beast* . . . with a twist. What will you do? How will you react? Your choices guide the story. Will your fairy tale be a dream come true, or will it turn into a nightmare?

Chapter One sets the scene. Then you choose which path to read. Follow the directions at the bottom of the page as you read the stories. The decisions you make will change your outcome. After you finish one path, go back and read the others for new perspectives and more adventures.

CHAPTER 1

A BEAUTIFUL BEAST

You stand in a strange place, but you are not alone. Someone—or something—lurks nearby. You hear the sound of scraping feet. You can smell the decay. And then you see it. The beast looks terrifying. But is it friend or foe? You cannot be sure.

As the saying goes, beauty is only skin deep. What does appearance really tell you? Imagine a rose. It represents everything that is beautiful, but its beauty is temporary. The rose dries. It wilts. It dies. Like the rose, your time is running out. The figure in the shadows draws closer. It is coming. You must decide if there is beauty behind the beast.

9

TO EXPERIENCE THE CLASSIC FAIRY TALE AS A BRAVE KNIGHT,
TURN TO PAGE 11.

TO BLAST INTO SPACE FOR A FUTURISTIC FAIRY TALE,
TURN TO PAGE 41.

TO CHASE YOUR DREAMS OF SUPERSTARDOM IN A MODERN TALE,
TURN TO PAGE 75.

CHAPTER 2

BURLEY AND THE BEAST

The Rose. You've pictured it in your mind hundreds of times. You've never seen the legendary sword up close, but you've heard tales of it since you were young. It is every knight's dream to find it. As you stare at the massive cave in front of you, it feels like it is finally within reach.

Even now, you think of your father and brothers. They are all accomplished knights. Your father served the king. Your oldest brother slayed a dragon. Even your little brother won a jousting tournament. But what have you done?

11

You may be a strong and brave knight, but that's not enough. You want to make your mark. Finding the Rose will make you a legend.

You've tracked the Rose for years. And now you believe you know where it rests. Here. You step into the cave. The entrance is covered in thick, mossy vines. Its dark tunnels twist and turn like a maze. You've heard tales of knights who have entered this place and never returned.

You brush the vines aside with the steel gloves that cover your hands. You wear a suit of armor that creaks and clangs as you step inside. Deeper and deeper you go into the cave. You're alone, yet you cannot shake the feeling that you're being watched.

"It's just nerves, Burley," you tell yourself.

The path takes you underground. You follow
as it twists and turns, leading to dead ends
and forks that double back on themselves. Yet
somehow the way seems clear to you. The Rose
is down here somewhere—you can feel it.

Minutes pass. Maybe hours. Down here,
time has little meaning. Finally, you turn a corner.
The tunnel opens to a chamber. The chamber
is huge. It could easily fit a thousand knights
inside—with room to spare. And there in the
center, a rose-colored sword sits on top of a
stone altar.

"The Rose," you whisper to yourself. You
step into the chamber. Your footsteps echo as
you walk toward the sword. You look around for
guards or booby traps. Nothing.

13

TURN THE PAGE.

This is too easy, you think.

You reach for the top of the sword. It fits your hand perfectly, as if it was made for you. You lift the huge sword from the stone, amazed at how light it feels. A large grin spreads across your face. You've done it! You can hardly wait to tell your father.

Suddenly you hear a growl behind you. You whirl around with the Rose in your hand. There, a great beast stands before you. You've never seen anything like it before. It towers over you. The beast is covered in thick, matted fur. Its face looks like a cross between a wolf and a person . . . a woman.

"I see you have plucked my Rose," growls the beast. It stands on the balls of its feet. Its claws dig into the ground, ready to attack.

TO RUN AWAY FROM THE BEAST, TURN TO PAGE 16.

TO ATTACK THE BEAST, TURN TO PAGE 18.

Clutching the Rose, you turn and run down the nearest tunnel. You twist and turn through the path. You can hear the sound of scraping claws. The beast is right behind you.

You hurry around a bend and see a stone staircase. You climb the stairs two at a time and reach the top. It leads to a long hallway. You reach the end and look around, gasping for breath. It's a dead end. There's no way out.

The scraping sound stops. You slowly turn around, knowing what you will see. The beast stands before you.

"The Rose is not yours to pluck," the beast says angrily. "Put down my father's sword at once!"

You're trapped. You look down at the Rose in your hand. It's not too late to attack. But maybe you can reason with the beast.

TO ATTACK THE BEAST, TURN TO PAGE 18.

TO TRY TALKING TO THE BEAST, TURN TO PAGE 19.

The beast stares at you with black eyes. The hairs on its giant arms stand on end. The huffing sound of its breath fills the room. You are sure the beast will shred you to ribbons at any moment.

You launch yourself at the beast, the sword clutched tightly in your grasp. You hack and slash with all your might, but the beast is lightning quick. She seems to know your every move before you make it. The beast ducks and dodges the sword with ease. You start to grow tired.

TO PUT DOWN YOUR SWORD AND SURRENDER, TURN TO PAGE 28.

TO CONTINUE YOUR ATTACK, TURN TO PAGE 30.

"I'm sorry," you say, gently placing the sword on the ground. "I didn't know the sword was yours. I heard tales it was guarded by a bea– . . . I mean, someone. But I didn't believe them."

The beast smiles. "Well, no harm has been done. What is your name, brave knight?"

"Burley," you reply. With a deep breath, you step forward and extend your right hand. "And you are?"

"They once called me Jane, a long time ago." Jane shakes your hand.

"Hello, Jane," you say.

Now that the beast has a name, she seems less fearsome. Yes, Jane is terrifying, but she also seems more human. You look around. Tunnels lead in every direction. You don't know which one leads outside the cave.

"How do I get out of here, Jane?" you ask. "I'm afraid I'm hopelessly lost."

"No, you cannot leave," Jane says, shaking her head. "You are a prisoner now. But worry not, young Burley. I will treat you kindly."

"No, please. This has all been a mistake," you plead. "I swear, I will leave and never come back. I will tell no one of this place. You have my word!"

"No, Burley," Jane sighs. "You will remain here."

Anger flares up within you. "Just how do you plan to keep me here?" you yell. "Will you lock me up like some animal?"

20

"No, no. This is my cave," Jane says, leaning close. Her breath stinks of rotten fish. "It obeys my command, twisting and reshaping itself as I will it. No one can escape unless I allow it." Then Jane walks away.

Nonsense, you tell yourself. *There was a way in. Surely there's a way out.* As soon as you get the chance, you'll run out of here. Until then, you'll try to gain the beast's trust.

In the first few weeks, you see little of Jane. She comes and goes, bringing you food and water. She says little. You're free to move around the cave, but every path you take leads you back to the sword room. As the weeks stretch into months, Jane starts to spend more time with you. Desperately lonely, you find yourself looking forward to her visits. You hate to admit it, but she's quite pleasant—for a beast.

The two of you sit together in her throne room. It's beautifully decorated. It looks like a room fit for a princess, not a beast. It's filled with elegant paintings, silks, and fine jewelry.

"Where did you get all this?" you ask one day.

Jane sighs. "It was all mine, before . . ."

"Before you became a beast?" you ask.

"Yes, I was not always so hideous," she answers. "I was once a young woman. A hundred years ago, my father was king of this realm. I was a beautiful princess, but a bit spoiled and selfish."

You lean in. "What happened?"

"A terrible drought struck the land," Jane explains. "My father was desperate to save the kingdom." She continues. "One day a witch appeared at our castle. She promised that she could end the drought. My father struck a deal with her. She made it rain in exchange for a huge amount of gold. But my father was foolish. He broke the deal he made with the witch and refused to pay."

"But why were you cursed if your father broke the deal?" you ask curiously.

"The witch knew that my father treasured two things in life above all others—his sword and his daughter," says Jane. "So as a punishment, she cursed me. I will remain a monster until someone loves me for who I am on the inside. Until then, I must guard my father's sword."

Jane seems different when she talks of her old life. Perhaps her heart is growing soft. Now might be the perfect time to ask her to let you out. After all, she knows what it's like to be a prisoner. But you do feel sorry for her. Maybe you could help her somehow.

24

TO HELP JANE BREAK THE CURSE, TURN TO PAGE 25.

TO ASK JANE TO LET YOU GO, TURN TO PAGE 32.

Trapped as a beast for a hundred years? You can't imagine what it must be like for Jane. You have to find a way to save her.

"What if I could help you, Jane?" you ask. "I don't love you. But I have grown fond of you. Perhaps with time, that could become more."

Jane looks at you. For a moment, her face appears to change. You swear you saw a beautiful young princess.

"Why would you do this for me?" Jane asks. "After I've kept you here?"

You take her hand. "I'm a knight, Jane. I've sworn an oath to help those in need. You may be more in need than anyone I've ever met." Jane just stares at you. She's speechless.

25

TURN THE PAGE.

"But before I can help you, I need to go home," you say. "I need to tell my family that I'm alive. Let me go, and I promise to return."

Jane's face brightens. She gives you a wide, toothy grin. "Go and see your family, Burley. But make sure you return. Keep your promise."

"I will return, Jane," you promise.

Suddenly, the cave starts to change. The tunnels move and merge into themselves until there's just one leading out. You run through the tunnel.

26 Soon you are back above ground. You head straight home. During the journey home, your mind races. What will you tell your family? Will they even believe you? Will you keep your promise to Jane and return?

When you walk into your small home, your father instantly wraps you in his arms. You're a grown man and a knight, but he still makes you feel like a little boy. Your brothers are happy to see you too. It feels good to be home. You eat together, then you practice your swordsmanship with your brothers.

After two days, your time in the cave seems far away. Can you really go back there? Jane may never let you go again. You toss and turn in bed, wrestling with the decision.

27

TO KEEP YOUR PROMISE TO JANE, TURN TO PAGE 34.

TO STAY WITH YOUR FAMILY, TURN TO PAGE 38.

You cannot win. You step back and toss the sword away. It clangs loudly on the stone floor. The high, sharp sound rings off the chamber's walls. The beast stares at you intensely.

"Please, I beg you," you cry. "Don't eat me!"

"Eat you?" the beast asks. "Why would I eat you? What is your name, knight?"

"B . . . B . . . Burley," you stammer.

The beast moves closer. "Well?" it asks.

You shake your head, not understanding. "Well what?" you ask.

"I have asked you your name," the beast replies. "Will you not ask me mine?"

"You have a name?" you ask. "But you're a beast!"

The beast lowers her head, wounded by your answer. Her body slumps. It occurs to you that she just might have feelings too.

"Very well," she says sadly. "I shall be only a beast, then." She turns and starts to walk away.

"Wait," you shout. "Where are you going? What about me?"

The beast looks back over her shoulder. "Oh, foolish Burley. Like me, you will stay here as a prisoner forever. This is your home now."

THE END

29

TO FOLLOW ANOTHER PATH, TURN TO PAGE 9.

Your father always told you to never give up. You won't quit now. With a battle cry, you raise the sword above your head and charge forward once more.

30

"Stop," the beast growls. But you don't stop. You swing again and again. But no matter what you do, the beast is too fast.

You realize too late that the beast is toying with you. Finally it decides to end the game.

The beast's fist slams into your chest, sending you flying backward. You slam against the stone wall with a crunch, then slump to the floor. The last thing you see is the beast standing over you before it strikes you for the final time.

THE END

TO FOLLOW ANOTHER PATH, TURN TO PAGE 9.

Jane's face is sad. Her deep-set eyes well up with tears. There may never be a better time to talk your way out of this prison.

"Jane, I'm sorry about your curse," you say. "I'm sure that someone will love you someday. But I can't wait that long. My family needs me. Please, will you let me go?"

Jane flinches as though your words have wounded her. Her shoulders slump. A tear falls from her eye, disappearing into her thick, matted fur. She closes her eyes, breathes deeply, and gives a slight nod.

"You may go," she whispers.

"Thank you, thank you," you say. Without another word, you turn and run.

True to her word, Jane lets you go. The cave's tunnels start to twist and turn, giving you a clear path to leave. When you get outside, you take a deep breath of the fresh air and start your journey home.

Yet even when you're home, you are not able to enjoy your freedom. You dream of a sad beast, locked inside her own prison. She is always waiting for someone to save her. You know that person will never be you. You have failed Jane as a knight and as a friend.

THE END

TO FOLLOW ANOTHER PATH, TURN TO PAGE 9.

"I have to go," you tell your family the next morning. "Someone needs my help. I don't know when I will return."

They try to talk you out of it, but you stand firm. Your father pats you on the shoulder. "I'm proud of you, Burley," he says. "You truly are a knight. Take care of yourself."

On your way back to the cave, you think about your choice to return. It's the right thing to do.

Once inside the cave, Jane greets you warmly. "I am so happy you've returned," she says. "I wasn't sure I would see you again."

"Of course I returned," you say, clasping Jane's arm. "I'm a knight. My word is everything to me. And I really do want to help you."

The two of you spend your days together, taking long walks through the cave. You talk about art, music, and legends. You discover that Jane loves jokes. You try to make her laugh.

One day, you and Jane are in the throne room. Jane is telling you more about her life before the curse. She tells you about the dances she used to go to, the dresses she wore, and about her love of horses. You close your eyes and think about what she might have looked like. You imagine a young woman with long, dark hair and brown eyes. You feel like you can really see how she looked.

Eventually, you open your eyes and turn to Jane. What you see shocks you. Jane is no longer a beast. She has changed. She looks just like the woman you imagined!

Jane sees your face. "What is it?" she asks.

"Look in the mirror!" you shout excitedly. Jane turns to the mirror behind her and sees her face—her human face. She screams in shock and faints. As she falls to the ground, you catch her in your arms.

You know what has happened. You have fallen in love with Jane. Not with how she looks on the outside, but who she is on the inside. The curse has been broken. Jane opens her eyes.

"How am I going to explain all of this to my family?" you ask, smiling.

36

She smiles back. "We'll figure it out. Now get me out of this prison. I want to see the sun again." You and Jane walk out of the cave together and into your happily ever after.

THE END
TO FOLLOW ANOTHER PATH, TURN TO PAGE 9.

You feel sorry for Jane, but this is your home. Your family loves you. They need you here. You can't risk being stuck in that cave forever.

You feel guilty about breaking your promise to Jane. But after a few months, that guilt starts to fade. After a year, you don't even think about Jane. By the time you're old and gray, you're not even sure what happened in that cave was real.

Then one day it all comes back. You're at the local shop getting some armor repaired. Three young knights are inside bragging.

"We found the Rose!" a knight announces inside the store. "The sword is real!" The man shows it to you. You recognize the rose-colored sword right away.

"Tell me," you gasp. "How did you take it?"

"Ahh," says the knight. "The beast that guarded the sword was terrible. We fought it for three days straight. I defeated it only through my great skill!"

"Bah," spits one of the other knights. "Don't believe him. The beast barely moved. It didn't even try to defend itself. It looked like it had just given up."

You barely hear the rest of the conversation. Jane is dead. She died alone and brokenhearted, and it is your fault. You can never forgive yourself.

39

THE END
TO FOLLOW ANOTHER PATH, TURN TO PAGE 9.

CHAPTER 3

BEAUTY AND THE B-345T

"Warning! Warning! You are entering a forbidden zone!" Your spaceship's computer flashes the warning over and over again.

"Turn off the alarms," you order. The red flashing light stops and silence falls over your little spaceship.

As a space explorer, you follow the rules of intergalactic travel to the letter. Normally, you stay away from forbidden space zones. But your ship's engine is sputtering. If you don't land somewhere soon, you could be stranded in deep space—which means certain death.

41

A planet you've never seen before is straight ahead. It's the only one nearby.

"How did I get myself into this?" you ask yourself. The truth is, you didn't have much of a choice. Your father's shipping business is in trouble. Money has been tight. You used to take your little spaceship out cruising around the galaxy. Now you must look for mineral-rich asteroids to bring in extra money.

Your ship shakes as the engine sputters again. The blue crystals that power your ship are failing. You just hope they last long enough to get you to the planet.

You look out the window of your ship. The unknown planet is green and blue with wispy purple clouds. "Clean air, perfect temperature, this place is perfect!" you say to yourself. "Ship, take us down."

You hold your breath as your ship enters the planet's atmosphere. If the engine fails now, you'll crash into the ground below. But you're in luck—the engine holds on. You feel only a small jolt as the ship's landing gear touches down.

"Ship, send out an emergency distress call," you say.

"Sending distress call," replies a computerized voice. "The call will take one Earth year to reach the nearest planet."

You groan. "I guess I'm on my own for a while," you say. You grab your hoverboard and laser blaster, open the hatch, and step outside.

The air outside is warm and comfortable. You hear the call of a bird echo in the distance. "My goodness, it's lovely here," you say.

You step on your board and hover over the ground, which is covered in a furry substance that looks like thick grass. In the distance, you see some sort of castle. It's tall and surrounded by a thick forest. You turn your board toward it. Maybe someone lives there who can help you.

As you get closer, you realize the castle is huge—it's taller than the tallest skyscraper on Earth. A great, oval doorway stands at the base of the castle. You clutch your laser blaster with both hands as you move toward the doorway. You've never actually used your blaster before. But your father insists that you take it with you any time you leave Earth.

Suddenly, a tall android emerges from the doorway. It's human-shaped but metallic. A gold crown sits atop its head and a red cape flaps behind its back.

The android's head turns and two glowing red eyes stare down at you.

TO TALK TO THE FIGURE, TURN TO PAGE 46.

TO FIRE YOUR LASER BLASTER AND RUN, TURN TO PAGE 71.

Your heart thumps in your chest. The android is huge. It stands before you, as still as a statue. It gives off a low hum, and its body crackles with electricity. You take a few steps forward.

"Hello," you say, extending your hand. "I'm Betty from planet Earth."

The android cocks its head slightly to one side. Its bright-red eyes dim slightly, then they turn to a cool blue.

"I am B-345T," it says. "But you may call me B-3. You have entered the realm of the Grimm Empire. Please come with me." It turns and marches back through the large doorway.

46

TO FOLLOW B-3, TURN TO PAGE 47.

TO RUN BACK TO YOUR SHIP, TURN TO PAGE 59.

You stand, afraid to move for a moment. The android disappears inside the castle, leaving you there.

Come on, Betty, you think. *You can do this.*

You take a deep breath and step through the giant doorway. Inside, the castle glows in a blue light. The walls and floor are giant slabs of stone. It looks like a cold, lonely place.

"Come," says the android. He raises his arm and points toward a giant chair. You have to pull yourself up onto the seat. As you sit there, you feel like a tiny child. The android sits in a second chair with a metallic clank.

"How have you come to my planet?" B-3 asks.

"My ship's power crystals failed," you explain. "This was the closest planet I could find. I barely made it here."

"Your ship has no power?" B-3 asks.

"No, not enough to get home," you reply sadly. "Maybe not even enough to get off this planet."

"You require help," says the android, its eyes blinking red. "I am programmed to assist anyone in need. I am sorry, but we do not have power crystals on this planet. But you may remain here as a . . . guest . . . of the Grimm Empire. I will care for you."

Something about the way B-3 said this makes you feel uneasy. You decide to keep him talking.

48

"This empire you mentioned," you say, "tell me about it."

B-3 leans in. "The Grimm were the first to live in this galaxy. They were storytellers. They passed down tales of adventure from generation to generation.

"And where are they now?" you ask.

B-3's eyes glow pink. "Unknown."

"Unknown?" you ask. "You have no idea where they are? How long have you been here alone?"

B-3's shoulders droop. "I have waited for their return for 286.4 million years."

"All alone?" you gasp.

"Yes," says the android, as his eyes dim to a soft white. "I was built to function for long periods of time without maintenance. But the last 100 million years have been lonely." B-3 looks at you hopefully. "Perhaps we could play a game? I have many, but they all require two players."

49

TURN THE PAGE.

You could be stuck here for a year by the time your distress call reaches help. Do you really want to spend all that time playing games with a giant android? You'd like to get a closer look at the castle. Maybe there's something here you could use to repair your ship.

TO AGREE TO A GAME, TURN TO PAGE 51.

TO DISTRACT B-3 AND LOOK AROUND, TURN TO PAGE 53.

You spend the rest of the day playing board games with a giant android. At first B-3 suggests ones meant for toddlers. You quickly explain that's more than a little insulting. Then he teaches you a game similar to checkers. You teach him how to play poker. He loves it but is terrible.

"Your eyes blink red every time you bluff," you say with a laugh.

"What does it mean to bluff?" B-3 asks.

"It means to lie," you answer. B-3 makes a strange clunking sound. You realize he's laughing.

"It feels good to talk to someone," the android **51** tells you. "Even androids need friends. You are my friend."

TURN THE PAGE.

The following day, you return to your ship to grab a few things. The ship's voice greets you. "Hello, Betty. I received a message to cancel the distress call. Can you confirm?"

You freeze. "What? No! Don't cancel the distress call. I'll be stuck here forever! Who sent that message?"

"Unknown," answers the computer.

"Play back the recording of the command," you say. You listen to the recording, and the voice is unmistakable. It's B-3. A sudden realization hits you. You're not a guest here. You're a prisoner.

52

TO CONFRONT B-3, TURN TO PAGE 56.

TO TRY TO ESCAPE THIS PLANET, TURN TO PAGE 62.

You think quickly. "I'm too hungry to play right now," you lie. "Do you have anything here that Earthlings can eat?"

B-3's eyes glow brighter. He seems eager to help. "Of course, I know just the thing," he says. "Unfortunately, it's a long journey to collect food. I'll be gone for much of the day."

You try not to smile. "Thank you so much, B-3."

When the android is gone, you start exploring the castle grounds. "Let's see what I can find here," you say to yourself.

The castle is huge. The rooms are two to three **53** times larger than anyone on Earth would build. The people who built them must have been giants.

On the far side of the castle, you come across a long, winding staircase. It spirals around the outside of the castle.

You climb the stairs to the very top. The top of the castle is wide and flat. You wonder if the Grimm landed their ships here. You notice a hatch.

Maybe this leads back inside the castle, you think.

The hatch is heavy, but you manage to lift it. The hatch covers a small storage room. You look inside, and what you see takes your breath away. The entire room is filled with glowing power crystals!

Only a handful of these crystals would power your ship and get you back home. You can't wait to tell B-3 the good news.

You freeze. "Hold on a second," you say. "B-3 told me there were no power crystals here. Why would he lie?"

You know the answer. B-3 has no intention of letting you leave.

TO CONFRONT B-3 ABOUT THE CRYSTALS, TURN TO PAGE 56.

TO TAKE THE POWER CRYSTALS, TURN TO PAGE 67.

"That no-good, lying android!" you growl. You turn around and march back inside the castle. The android is back with a cart of fruit. He watches as you approach. He seems to sense your mood. His eyes turn a dim gray.

"Am I a guest or a prisoner here, B-3?" you demand, your voice shaking with anger.

B-3's eyes start to blink red. It reminds you of the poker game. You know he's about to lie to you.

"You are my guest," B-3 bluffs.

"You're lying to me!" you shout angrily. "Why are you keeping me here?"

The android's massive shoulders slump. His eyes stop blinking. "I am sorry, Betty. I want to help you, but I can't let you leave. I am so lonely."

"You can't do this, B-3!" you shout. "You can't make me stay here because you're lonely! I need to be with my family on my own planet."

B-3 kneels down, bringing his eyes down to your level. "Come now. Let's play a game. It will be fun."

"No!" you shout. "I won't be your prisoner. If you are my friend, prove it. Let me go. Let me tell my family that I'm OK."

B-3 seems to think this over. "If I let you go, you must promise two things," he finally says. "First, you must keep this planet—and me—a secret. You must never tell anyone."

"OK," you reply. "I can do that. What else?"

"Secondly," B-3 continues, "You must return to play games with me."

You nod. "I promise I'll return, B-3."

The android rises. "Then let's go to your ship. I can repair it for you quite easily."

It takes B-3 less than an hour to replace your power crystals. As your ship starts to lift off, he stands back and waves. You chart a course for Earth and speed away.

When you get home, your father wraps you up in a bear hug. "Where have you been all this time?" he asks.

TO TELL YOUR FATHER EVERYTHING, TURN TO PAGE 64.

TO KEEP YOUR PROMISE TO B-3, TURN TO PAGE 66.

A chill runs down your spine. The thought of following a giant android anywhere fills you with dread.

"No way," you say. "I'm out of here!"

You hop onto your hoverboard and speed back to your ship as fast as it can carry you. Behind you, you can hear a buzzing sound. You look back toward the castle. The android is chasing you!

"Ship!" you shout into the communicator on your wrist. "Open the main door, now! Prepare for takeoff!"

"Opening main door," the ship's voice replies. "Be advised that current power crystal levels are low."

"Just do it!" you shout.

You hop off your hoverboard and run up the ramp into the ship. The android is only a few seconds behind. You quickly close the main door.

"Ship, get us out of here!" you cry.

The ship rises and speeds away. You watch the castle disappear over the horizon. You finally breathe easy after it disappears. Just then, the ship shudders. A loud, piercing whistle screams out from the engine.

"Power loss critical," reports the ship. "Emergency landing required." Your ship touches down on another part of the planet.

"Where are we?" you ask the ship. There's no response. The ship's power is drained. You look outside. The ship has landed in a swamp. It's slowly sinking down into the muck.

Grabbing your board, you bail out—just in time to watch your ship disappear.

You stare in disbelief. You may have escaped the swamp, but you can't leave the planet without your ship. And no one knows where you are. You're trapped here.

THE END
TO FOLLOW ANOTHER PATH, TURN TO PAGE 9.

61

"Ship," you call out, "how much power do we have left in our power crystals?"

"Power is dangerously low," replies the ship's voice.

"It will have to be enough," you say. "Power up, ship. Take us into space now!"

"I cannot recommend this," the ship replies. "The odds of safely going into space are less than . . . ."

"Do it now!" you bark.

The ship's engine whirs to life, but it doesn't sound right. You know this ship better than anything, and you know that the engine is dying. But you don't care. If you don't escape now, you don't know if you'll get another chance.

The ship rises above the ground, then rapidly climbs into the sky. You look out your window, watching the castle disappear beneath you. Suddenly, an alarm begins to wail. The engine shudders, then turns off. The ship begins to fall. You watch as the ground rushes back up toward you. Now you'll never leave this alien planet.

THE END
TO FOLLOW ANOTHER PATH, TURN TO PAGE 9.

You remember your promise to B-3. But you've had an incredible adventure. What's the harm in telling one person? And this is your father. He was probably worried sick about you. He deserves to know where you've been. You tell your father the whole story.

"I know it sounds unbelievable, Dad," you say, "but it's all true! It was the adventure of a lifetime!"

"I'm so glad you're safe," your father says, picking up his communicator. "We have to tell the intergalactic police about this right away!"

A flash of panic washes over you. "No, wait!" you say, reaching for him. "B-3 said we couldn't tell anyone!"

"Of course that no-good bucket of bolts would say that," says your father. "I know you've been through a lot. Let me handle this."

In the weeks that follow, you watch it all unfold on the news—an unknown planet, an alien android, intergalactic police flying off for battle.

"This is the view from space," says the newscaster on TV. "Even from here, you can make out the large size of the alien castle. The intergalactic police have seen signs that the android is the only one on the planet." The newscaster continues. "Now, you can see the orange glow building up around the police ship. That is the space laser powering up. Look at that! The laser has completely destroyed the alien castle. This new planet is now safe for humans to colonize. The alien threat has been destroyed."

You put your head into your hands and cry. "What have I done?"

THE END
TO FOLLOW ANOTHER PATH, TURN TO PAGE 9.

65

"I . . . um . . . I just got lost," you say to your father. "My communicator wasn't working. I'm sorry you were worried."

Your father nods and hugs you again. And just like that, life is back to normal. A few weeks later, you return to the alien planet. B-3 greets you as you touch down just outside the castle.

"I am so pleased to see you, my friend!" B-3 says. "Come, come! I have many games for us to play!"

You smile. You have the most interesting friend in the galaxy.

66

THE END
TO FOLLOW ANOTHER PATH, TURN TO PAGE 9.

You hurry back inside the castle. Soon B-3 is back with a cart full of fruit. "These should be healthy and tasty," he says.

You start to eat. "It is so wonderful having you here," B-3 tells you. "I spend so much of my time just staring at the stars, wishing for my people to return. I play games of chance with myself. But games are more fun with a friend. Perhaps we could play one now?"

You shrug your shoulders and agree. You will have to wait for the right time to go after the power crystals. You don't want to make B-3 suspicious.

You spend the day playing games. B-3 tries to teach you some of the games he knows, but you're distracted. Your mind keeps going back to those power crystals. So instead, you teach the android how to play chess.

"What a truly marvelous game!" B-3 exclaims. "The possible moves are endless! I must introduce this chess to the Grimm when they return!"

Several days pass, and you're growing restless. "B-3," you ask one morning, "I'm growing tired of this food. Do you think you could find me something new? Maybe something from another part of the planet?"

B-3's eyes glow a warm yellow. You can tell he's excited to help you. "There is a type of melon that grows only in the mountains to the far west," he explains. "I will bring you some. I shall return before nightfall."

When he's gone, you get to work. You pull the cart that B-3 used to bring you food up the long staircase. Then you use some cable from your ship to make a pulley at the top of the tower.

It's hard work, but you manage to use the pulley to haul some of the power crystals up and out of the storage room. Carefully you load them into the cart. You push the cart down the steps, one thud at a time.

The sun is low in the sky by the time you reach the entrance of the castle.

"I better hurry," you say to yourself. "B-3 will be back soon."

You roll the cart of power crystals to your ship as fast as you can. It only takes a few minutes to plug in the new crystals.

"New power crystals detected," says the ship. "Ready for takeoff."

"Start the engine, ship!" you blurt out.

You look out the window as the ship rises into the air. As it turns, you spot a figure standing in a clearing. B-3 carries a large basket filled with melons. Just before B-3 disappears from sight, the glow in his eyes disappears completely.

THE END
TO FOLLOW ANOTHER PATH, TURN TO PAGE 9.

70

A giant android! In a panic, you point your laser blaster toward the hulking figure and pull the trigger. Bright blue shoots from the blaster and hits the android's shoulder.

The blast spins the android around, but it recovers quickly. Its eyes glow a bright, blinding white. Suddenly twin beams of white light shoot from its eyes. You hurl yourself out of the way just in time. The beams strike a small bush behind you, which catches fire.

71

TURN THE PAGE.

You whirl around and fire at the android again. Direct hit! But the beam barely seems to slow it down. The android marches toward you, eyes glowing white. As its shadow falls over you, you realize that you won't have time to shoot your laser again. The android's eyes glow as it fires again. This time, it doesn't miss.

THE END
TO FOLLOW ANOTHER PATH, TURN TO PAGE 9.

CHAPTER 4

THE BEAUTIFUL MUSIC

"I just can't do it anymore, Dad," you say into your phone as you walk down the street. "I sang my heart out today, and the judges barely looked at me. All they said was, 'We'll get back to you.' You know what that means in an audition, Dad? It means 'take a hike.'"

"Now, Annabelle," says your dad. "You've wanted to be a singer ever since you were a little girl. It's not easy, but nothing worth doing ever is. Come home and we'll . . ." The call cuts off before he can finish. You look at your screen.

75

"Dead battery," you groan, jamming the phone into your pocket. "Just my luck."

Your stomach growls as you reach your bus stop. You were so nervous about your audition that you didn't eat all day. You glance at your watch—six minutes until the bus arrives. You look around. There's a taco stand half a block away. There's just enough time.

Just as you're about to take a bite of your piping-hot tofu taco, you hear it. The *hiss* of the bus as it comes to a stop.

"Oh no!" you shout, dropping your taco on the ground. You run down the street, waving at the bus. But it's too late. You watch helplessly as it rolls away and disappears. There isn't another bus scheduled for an hour. You start walking. Maybe a brisk walk is what you need on a day like today.

"It's not like it can get any worse," you mutter to yourself.

That's when the first clap of thunder shakes the ground. You look up. The sky is dark gray. Then the rain starts. It pours down in sheets. Flashes of lightning fill the sky, and the wind begins to howl.

You cover your face, searching for somewhere to take shelter. There's nothing around—just old, abandoned buildings. The rain stings your eyes as you walk. You try to open the doors of a few buildings along the street. But everything is locked up tight.

At the end of the block stands a large, three-story house. The place looks ancient. A broken fence circles around an overgrown lawn.

You try to peek into one of the cracked windows but can't reach. The storm is getting stronger, so you throw yourself into the front door. To your surprise, it starts to move. You hit it again with the side of your hip, and it opens.

Inside, it takes a moment for your eyes to adjust. You look around and gasp. This house may have looked like an abandoned dump on the outside. But inside it looks like a palace! Beautiful artwork hangs on the walls. A large oak dining set stands in the next room, polished and clean. You find yourself staring in disbelief. But the sound of footsteps gets your attention.

"Hello?" calls a voice. "What do you think you are doing in here?"

A figure steps out of the darkness. It's a young man, dressed in designer jeans and an expensive-looking shirt.

He looks about your age. Thick, dark hair spills over his shoulders. A bushy beard reaches down to his chest. His thick eyebrows seem to be swallowing his face. He walks toward you.

TO APOLOGIZE FOR BREAKING IN, TURN TO PAGE 80.

TO GRAB THE PEPPER SPRAY IN YOUR POCKET, TURN TO PAGE 82.

"Hello," you say. Your heart races and your hands tremble. You take a deep breath. "I'm sorry for coming inside your . . . house. I thought this building was abandoned. I was just trying to find a dry place to wait out the storm."

The young man looks irritated. "As you can see, it's not abandoned. This is my home."

"Yes, I'll be on my way," you say. "Could I possibly use your cell phone to call a cab? My phone is dead."

"Cell phone? Sorry, I don't own one," the young man says.

"No phone?" you say in disbelief. "Who doesn't have a phone?"

The young man smirks. It's a warm expression that leaves you feeling a little more comfortable.

"Look at you," he says. "You're soaking wet. Since it doesn't look like you plan to rob me, come and sit by the fire. It will warm you."

You hesitate. This man seems nice, but he is a stranger. You glance back over your shoulder as the storm rages outside. Right on cue, a bright flash of lightning rips across the sky, followed by a ground-rattling crash of thunder. You can't go back out in that. You're stuck here.

TO FOLLOW THE YOUNG MAN TO THE FIRE, TURN TO PAGE 84.

TO REMAIN CLOSE TO THE FRONT DOOR, TURN TO PAGE 86.

You whisk the bottle of pepper spray from
your pocket and point it at the young man's face.

"Stay back!" you shout.

He throws up his hands to cover his face. "Whoa, hold on!" he yells. "What are you doing? You break into my house and threaten me with pepper spray? I'm just trying to help you!"

He's right. He didn't ask you to come inside. You have no right to threaten him inside his own home. You slip the bottle of pepper spray back into your pocket.

TO INTRODUCE YOURSELF, TURN TO PAGE 84.

TO LEAVE NOW, TURN TO PAGE 104.

After you get a better look at the young man, you can't shake the feeling you've seen him before. You step forward and introduce yourself.

"I'm Annabelle," you say, extending your hand.

"I'm Trey," he replies. "It's nice to meet you, Annabelle. Come, the fire is warm."

You follow Trey down a hallway and into an open living area. The room is beautifully decorated, with a large leather sofa and a slate coffee table. A fire crackles in a large, ornate fireplace. A guitar lies on the floor nearby. Both of you sit by the fire. After a while, you try to break the silence.

"Do you play?" you ask, pointing to the guitar.

"Sometimes, to pass the time," Trey says. "How about you?"

"Oh yes," you say. "I sing and play guitar. Actually, I was on my way home from an audition when I got caught in the storm."

"How did it go?" Trey asks.

"Not great," you say honestly. Suddenly, another clap of thunder crashes outside. Trey looks up.

"It sounds like we'll be here for awhile. Maybe we could play a song together. I'll play and you sing," he says, grabbing the guitar.

You start to feel very nervous. Sing for a complete stranger? Your chest tightens up at the thought.

85

TO SING WITH TREY, TURN TO PAGE 92.

TO SAY NO, TURN TO PAGE 103.

"Umm thanks, but I think I'll stay right here," you say, backing away.

"Suit yourself," the young man says softly. His deep-gray eyes look sad. "You may stay here if you wish to wait out the storm."

With a slight bow, he turns and disappears back into the shadows. You are alone. Outside, you hear the wind howling. The rain batters the side of the run-down house. It seems like the storm will never end.

Suddenly, a new sound drifts toward you from inside the building. It's a voice and a guitar. Soft notes carry through the air. You can barely make out the lyrics, but you've heard the song before. It is a ballad about lost love and missed opportunities. It's beautiful. Your heart aches at the lyrics and the melody.

Is it a radio? It couldn't be the young man making such beautiful music, could it? Outside, the rain has stopped. You can leave any time you wish.

TO SEARCH FOR THE MUSIC, TURN TO PAGE 88.

TO LEAVE NOW, TURN TO PAGE 96.

That song . . . . You're sure you've heard it before. You just can't remember where. You calm your nerves and walk through the beautiful house, following the sound. Finally you round a corner, where a warm orange glow flickers throughout the room.

The young man sits in front of the fire, strumming his guitar as he sings. His eyes are closed, and he is unaware of your presence. As he sings, you remember the name of the song—"My Rose." It was a huge hit a few years ago. You imagine what the song would sound like as a duet. You close your eyes and start to sing.

The man doesn't miss a beat. He softens his voice, letting yours rise. You sing together, letting your voices build off each other as the song takes on a life of its own. It's magical.

As the man strums the final chords on his guitar, the room falls silent. The two of you just stare at each other. Then his face breaks out into a huge grin.

"It's been a long time since I've sung that song," he says. "I've always felt like something was missing. Now I know what it was. It was you. This song was never a solo. It was a duet."

You stare at the man. In your mind, you peel away the scruffy beard and long hair. And suddenly, you can see it.

"Wait a second," you say. "You're Trey Johnson! The most famous pop star ever to disappear off the face of the earth."

Trey smiles and nods.

"What are you doing here? What happened to you?" you ask.

Trey shrugs. "I became famous so fast. I wasn't ready. All the attention, the photographers, the fans—I couldn't take it. I had panic attacks. So I just disappeared. Somewhere nobody would find me."

"This is a good place to hide," you say.

Trey nods. You sit beside the warm fire and continue to talk. Time gets away from you. At one point, you look at your watch.

"Oh no," you gasp. "My father is going to be worried sick. I have to go."

"Will you come back?" Trey asks. "Will you sing with me again?"

TO AGREE TO COME BACK, TURN TO PAGE 94.

TO STAY AWAY, TURN TO PAGE 101.

You want to be a singer. How can you be afraid to sing in front of someone you barely know? You take a deep breath and start to sing your favorite song—"My Rose." Your voice cracks a few times, but you put everything you have into it.

When you hit the chorus, Trey joins in. He strums his guitar gently as he echoes your lyrics. His voice is deep and smooth. It seems to cut right into your soul.

He may look like a beast, you think, *but his voice is beautiful.* As you sing the final note, you open your eyes. Trey is smiling back at you.

"That was wonderful," he says. "When I wrote that song, I never knew how great it could sound as a duet."

"Wait, you wrote 'My Rose'?" you ask. Then you make the connection. "Wait, you're Trey Johnson! I love your music."

The two of you sit by the fire for hours. Trey tells you about his days as a pop star and how he left it all behind when it got to be too much. You sing and talk and sing some more. It's like magic.

"I have to get going," you tell Trey. "The storm has passed, and my dad will be worried."

"Would you like to sing together again?" Trey asks you as you gather your things.

It's been fun singing together, and your voices blend wonderfully. But you have dreams of superstardom, and Trey ran away from his chance in the spotlight. How can he help you?

93

TO AGREE TO SING AGAIN, TURN TO PAGE 94.

TO SAY NO, TURN TO PAGE 103.

You don't hesitate. "Of course I'll come back," you promise. You cannot wait to sing with Trey again.

"But please," Trey adds, "don't tell anyone I'm here. All the reporters—I couldn't bear it."

"Your secret is safe with me," you say with a smile.

You half-walk, half-run the rest of the way home. When you finally walk through the front door, your dad is upset.

"Do you have any idea how worried I was?" your dad asks. "Where were you?"

You tell your dad about the storm, your dead cell phone, taking shelter inside the three-story house, and the kindly stranger. But you keep Trey's secret. You don't tell your dad the owner of the house was once one of the biggest pop stars on the planet.

Your eyes shine with excitement as you tell the tale. But when you're finished, your dad is furious.

"You spent the day with a complete stranger?" he roars. "Are you crazy? I hope you don't plan on going back there again. Because I forbid it!"

You've never seen your dad so upset. It shakes you. What if he's right? I mean, Trey may be famous, and you felt a real connection to him, but you don't really know him.

95

TO IGNORE YOUR DAD'S WISHES AND RETURN, TURN TO PAGE 98.

TO LISTEN TO YOUR DAD, TURN TO PAGE 101.

The music sounds beautiful. But you're more than a little freaked out by this strange house and its even stranger owner. You listen a moment longer. Then you step outside onto the soaked sidewalk. You find yourself singing the song as you walk the rest of the way home.

Months pass. Soon the storm, the house, and the young man are only memories. Then one day you're riding the bus to another audition. As you listen to the radio on your phone, it all comes rushing back to you. That voice. That song. You hold your breath, listening to it, remembering.

"That was Trey Johnson," says the radio announcer. "You may remember him from a few years ago when he burst onto the music scene, only to disappear completely. Well he's back, and he's the hottest thing in pop music right now."

It takes you a moment to put it together. "Did I really meet Trey Johnson?" you ask yourself.

It's unbelievable and heartbreaking. You had a chance to get to know him—maybe even sing with him—but you let your fear stop you. Instead, you're just another fan listening to his beautiful music.

THE END
TO FOLLOW ANOTHER PATH, TURN TO PAGE 9.

There's no way your dad could understand. You can't blame him for wanting to protect you, but it's Trey Johnson! Chances to sing with a pop star don't just come along every day.

So the next day, when your dad is at work, you grab your guitar and make your way back to Trey's house. When you arrive, you are greeted by a FOR SALE sign in the yard.

"Trey!" you shout as you knock on the door. "Trey, I'm back!" But no one answers. You peer through a window. The house is empty.

Trey is gone. You slump to the ground. It feels like you've been punched in the stomach. How could he just leave? He told you to come back, right? Did you just imagine the whole thing?

You wipe the tears from your eyes and stand up to collect yourself. That's when you see the small note taped to the front door.

Annabelle,

Meet me at 545 Main Street at noon. Let's make some music.

—Trey

You look at your watch—it's 11:30 a.m. You have to hurry. You run to a busier street, hail a taxi, and rush to the address. The sign above the building reads *ARCH RECORDS*. Trey stands in front of the building, waiting for you. He shaved off his beard and cut his hair. He looks like the old Trey Johnson from your album covers. He welcomes you with open arms.

TURN THE PAGE.

"I knew you'd come," he says. "I never told you this, but I've been trying to finish my new album for months. It always felt one song short. Now, I know I have that song. What do you say, are you ready to become a rock star?"

100

All you can do is grin.

THE END
TO FOLLOW ANOTHER PATH, TURN TO PAGE 9.

Trey may have been a pop star once upon a time, but he's been out of the music scene for years. Now he's living alone in a house like a hermit, hiding from everyone. That's not normal. It's best to keep your distance.

Then one day, you walk by his house. It's boarded up and a FOR SALE sign stands by the front door. Trey is long gone. Any chance you had to sing with him again is gone too. You tell yourself that you made the right decision.

After a few months, the memory of that night and Trey fades. That is until the radio brings it all back.

"Our next song comes from Trey Johnson," says the radio announcer. "Yes, THAT Trey Johnson. He's back! And here's his latest song, "Annabelle."

All your friends are obsessed with Trey Johnson and his new hit. You tell them you are the Annabelle from the song, but they never believe you. Now every time you hear it, you wonder if you'd be singing the song with him if you had made a different choice.

THE END
TO FOLLOW ANOTHER PATH, TURN TO PAGE 9.

"No, no," you stammer. "I'm not very good. I wanted to be a singer, but I don't have what it takes."

Trey shrugs. "Suit yourself," he says. "Here, sit by the fire. It'll keep you warm until the storm passes."

The two of you struggle to make small talk until the storm weakens. You can't wait to get out of there and go home.

Months later, you see a man singing on TV. You don't recognize him as the scruffy stranger you met that night. Trey Johnson becomes the hottest singer in the world. You're just a fan, like everyone else.

After that night, you realize that your dreams of 103 pop stardom are silly. You put away your guitar for good and focus on school. The only singing you do now is in the shower, where no one can judge you ever again.

THE END
TO FOLLOW ANOTHER PATH, TURN TO PAGE 9.

You don't want to pepper spray the man, but you know better than to stay in an abandoned house with a complete stranger. Gripping the bottle in your pocket, you back away.

"I'm going to go," you say.

The young man takes a step forward and extends a hand. "Don't be silly. It's not safe out there."

You don't feel safe in here either. Your hand trembles as you pull out the bottle of pepper spray. It all happens in a blur. The man flinches, and you press the button. The potent spray shoots out of the bottle, straight into the stranger's eyes. He yells and falls to the floor, clutching his face.

You turn and run out of the house as fast as you can. You don't even care about the raging storm. It's a long, miserable walk home. You're soaked to the bone when you burst through the door. You don't stop shivering the rest of the night, though not just from the cold.

You tell your friends the story about when you were almost attacked by a hairy beast. You always make the man sound bigger and meaner than he really was. Soon the night is a distant memory and you are preparing for another audition. Maybe you'll take a taxi there this time, just in case.

105

THE END

TO FOLLOW ANOTHER PATH, TURN TO PAGE 9.

A TALE AS OLD AS TIME

The story of *Beauty and the Beast* is a classic and beloved fairy tale. It tells the story of a young woman and the fearsome beast who keeps her a prisoner. The two strike up a friendship, and the beast puts his trust in the woman. Eventually he allows her to go home, after she promises that she will return. When she keeps her promise and comes back, the two fall in love.

No one knows for sure when or where the original *Beauty and the Beast* was written. Some people believe that the story is based on the real lives of Petrus and Catherine Gonsalvus, who lived in the 1500s. Petrus had a rare condition that left him covered in hair from his head to his toes. However, most believe that *Beauty and the Beast* is far older. One study suggests the tale is 4,000 years old.

The best-known version of the tale is based on a story written by Gabrielle-Suzanne Barbot de Villeneuve in 1740. The story, *La Belle et la Bête*, is about a young girl named Belle, who is captured by a beast. However in Villeneuve's tale, Belle has cruel sisters who torment her. Also, the beast is not clever and charming. He is dull and dim-witted. Belle does not fall in love with him—she feels sorry for him.

Many other versions of the tale exist. In an Italian version called *The Pig King*, the beast is a prince cursed to look like a pig until he marries three times. The prince marries and then kills two sisters. When he finally marries the third sister, the curse is lifted and the couple go on to rule the kingdom together.

Like most fairy tales, *Beauty and the Beast* has changed to reflect society's values. In recent years the story changed to make Beauty a hero rather than a victim. For example in the 2017 Disney movie *Beauty and the Beast*, Belle is portrayed as strong and independent. This is the Beauty that modern fans have come to know. Her story of bravery and heroism has helped to make *Beauty and the Beast* one of the most beloved fairy tales in the world.

OTHER PATHS TO EXPLORE

1. In Chapter 3, the android B-3 spent millions of years alone, waiting for the Grimm to return. How do you think B-3 felt when Betty came to his world? How would you feel? Do you think B-3 did the right thing trying to keep Betty there? Why or why not?

2. In Chapter 4, the fairy tale takes place in modern times. How is this version similar to the original fairy tale? How is it different? Imagine you were writing a new version of *Beauty and the Beast*. Where would it take place?

3. In the classic fairy tale *Beauty and the Beast*, Belle falls in love with the prince, even though he looks like a beast. What do you think the lesson is from this tale?

READ MORE

Braswell, Liz. *As Old as Time*. A Twisted Tale.
Los Angeles: Disney Press, 2016.

Mlynowski, Sarah. *Beauty Queen*. Whatever After.
New York: Scholastic Press, 2015.

Snowe, Olivia. *Beauty and the Basement*. Twicetold
Tales. North Mankato, Minn.: Stone Arch Books, 2014.

INTERNET SITES

Use FactHound to find Internet sites related to this
book.

Visit: www.facthound.com

Just type in 9781543530070 and go.

LOOK FOR OTHER BOOKS IN THIS SERIES: